SCOOBY-DOO!™

A Very SCARY VALENTINE'S DAY

DEVELOPING READER • LEVEL 2 • 250-750 WORDS

By Mariah Balaban
Illustrated by Duendes del Sur

WORLDWIDE PUBLISHING

SCHOLASTIC INC.
New York Toronto London Auckland
Sydney Mexico City New Delhi Hong Kong

ISBN 978-0-545-24983-6

Designed by Michael Massen

12 11 10 9 8   13 14 15/0

Printed in U.S.A.   40
First printing, December 2010

It was Valentine's Day, and the gang had stayed late after school.

Scooby and Shaggy were making cards for their friends.

Shaggy drew a picture of a banana split. "Valentine, I'm bananas over you!" he declared.

"Ree-hee-hee," Scooby giggled.

"Let's find the gang and give them their cards," said Shaggy.

Scooby and Shaggy wandered through the school.

"Like, it sure is creepy after school when nobody's around," Shaggy whispered. "I'd hate to run into any ghosts or ghoulies."

"Ruh-huh," Scooby-Doo agreed.

Shaggy and Scooby opened the door to the gym.
Fog filled the room.
Scooby whimpered.
Shaggy shivered.

"Is it just me, or is something funny going on?" Shaggy asked.

Suddenly, the lights started flashing on and off.

Scooby and Shaggy saw something spooky coming toward them!

"Yikes! That looks like a zombie!" Shaggy shouted.

"Rombie?" yelped Scooby-Doo.

"Let's get out of here!" cried Shaggy.

The zombie chased Scooby and Shaggy out into the hallway.
ARRRROOOOOR!
A scary moan filled the air.
Another zombie lurched toward them.

Scooby and Shaggy hid in an empty classroom.

"Phew!" Shaggy panted. "It looks like we lost him!"

They *had* lost that zombie, but found another!

11

A cloud of smoke filled the air.
The zombie was coming for them!
Shaggy scrambled for the door. "Like, class dismissed!"

"Zoinks!" exclaimed Shaggy. "The zombies
are everywhere! We have to find the gang
and save them!"

"Ret's ro!" barked Scooby.

Scooby and Shaggy decided to check the cafeteria.

"If we don't find the gang, at least we'll find a snack," said Shaggy.

Scooby's tummy rumbled in agreement.

Velma and Daphne were in the cafeteria.
"Velma! Daphne!" Shaggy called to them.
"Boy, are we glad to see you!"
Velma and Daphne turned around.
"Ruh-roh," said Scooby-Doo.

Velma and Daphne had turned into zombies!
"Like, on second thought, we'll take this
to go!" cried Shaggy, grabbing some fries.
"Run for it, Scoob!"

Scooby and Shaggy bolted from the cafeteria. *"Scooooooby, Shaaaaaaaggy!"* zombie Velma and zombie Daphne called after them. *"Cooooome baaaack!"*

Scooby and Shaggy kept running. They ran out the school doors, down the steps, and right into . . .
Fred!

"Fred!" Shaggy exclaimed. "The zombies got Velma and Daphne!"

"Are rou ra rombie, roo?" asked Scooby.

"Zombie?" laughed Fred. "I'm not a zombie. What's gotten into you two?"

"It all started in the gym," Shaggy explained. "We saw weird lights and a zombie in the spooky fog!"

"Weird lights and spooky fog?" Fred said. "I've been testing the fog machine and strobe lights for the Valentine's Day dance."

"And I'm no zombie!" a voice behind them cried.
Fred introduced Scooby and Shaggy to his friend
Carl. "Carl was helping me decorate the gym."

"I got all tangled up in a roll of streamers," Carl said. "Under the strobe light, I must have looked pretty creepy."

"You can say that again," Shaggy said.

"Well, what about the spooky moan we heard?" Shaggy asked.

Fred said that he had been testing the speaker system. "I guess it was echoing in the hallway."

"That doesn't explain the other zombies we saw," said Shaggy.

"I don't know about any zombies," said Mr. Wilson, the math teacher. "But I hit my thumb hanging these posters. I must have made some pretty mean-looking faces."

"And I was covered in white dust because I was cleaning erasers," said Bob, the janitor. "I bet that's why you thought I was a zombie!"

Scooby, Shaggy, and Fred headed back to the cafeteria to find Velma and Daphne.

"Velma! Daphne! You're okay!" exclaimed Shaggy.

"Of course we're okay," Daphne said. "No thanks to you guys."

"We needed your help cleaning up the punch we spilled," said Velma. "We called your names, but you just kept running."

"We thought you were zombies," said Shaggy. Everyone laughed.

Just then, Scooby and Shaggy remembered
the Valentine's Day cards.

"Scooby and I made these for you!" Shaggy
said proudly.

The gang loved their Valentine's Day cards.

Velma and Daphne had made something
for Shaggy and Scooby, too: heart-shaped
cookies!

"Like, this has turned out to be one
sweet Valentine's Day," Shaggy mumbled.

"Rappy Ralentine's Ray!" Scooby barked. Scooby-Dooby Doo!